SERIOUS FARM

Houghton Mifflin Company
Boston

TIM EGAN

To all my friends
at the Westwood Flower Garden

www.houghtonmifflinbooks.com

The text of this book is set in Century Oldstyle.
The illustrations are ink and watercolor on paper.

Library of Congress Cataloging-in-Publication Data

Egan, Tim.
Serious farm / Tim Egan.
p. cm.
Summary: Farmer Fred takes his work very seriously and so do his animals,
until they decide they need to make the farm more fun and set out to find a way
to make Farmer Fred laugh.
HC ISBN 0-618-22694-X   PAP ISBN 0-618-73745-6
[1. Farm life—Fiction. 2. Domestic animals—Fiction.] I. Title.
PZ7.E2815 Se 2003
[E]—dc21   2002151857

HC ISBN-13: 978-0-618-22694-8
PAP ISBN-13: 978-0-618-73745-1

Manufactured in China
SCP 10 9 8 7 6 5 4

Farmer Fred never smiled much. He wasn't a sad fellow, just very serious.
"Farmin' is serious business," he'd say. "Nothing funny about corn."

Now, because it was Farmer Fred's farm, all the animals acted like he did, so they were very serious, too.

When he would say, "There's no humor in tomatoes," they'd all agree.

The pigs, the cows, the horses, the chickens, the rabbit, the sheep.
All extremely serious.

One night, Edna, the cow, said, "We've got to get Farmer Fred to laugh.
I mean, it's okay to be serious, but not all the time. We need some laughter."
"Must admit," said Bernie, the goat, "I wouldn't mind smilin' again."

He stretched his mouth and showed all his teeth. It wasn't a very convincing smile. They all decided they needed a plan to make the farm more fun.

The next morning, as the sun came up, Edna was standing on the fence where Cormac, the rooster, usually stood.

She was barely able to keep her balance.

She tried to yell, "Cock-a-doodle-do," but since she was a cow, it didn't come out like that at all. It was the first time anyone had done anything funny in months, so it made all the animals laugh.

Farmer Fred just looked out the window and said, "You're not a rooster," and shut the window and went back to sleep.

"Wow," said Edna, "this is gonna be tougher than I thought."

That morning was serious as usual, with Farmer Fred saying things like
"Broccoli's no fun" and "I never laugh at bell peppers."
"Okay," said Edna to the others, "let's try another idea."

When Farmer Fred went to feed the pigs that afternoon, they started barking like dogs. Everyone thought it was hilarious but Farmer Fred.

"That's more weird than funny," he said as he walked away.

"All right," said Edna, "this isn't working. Let's try something new."

They sneaked into the house and took some clothes from Farmer Fred's closet and put them on. It wasn't as easy as it sounds.

That evening, as the moon lit up the field, Bernie rang the doorbell. Farmer Fred came out onto the porch and said, "What in the world?" The animals were all dancing around in Farmer Fred's clothes.

They were terrible dancers, which actually made it funnier. But Farmer Fred just said, "Better not get my clothes dirty."
He walked back inside without smiling.

For the next two weeks, the animals tried everything they could to make Farmer Fred smile a little, but nothing worked.

It got to be very discouraging.

One night, the animals met in the barn.

"Well, I don't know about you," said Edna, "but I can't take it anymore. I have to live somewhere more fun than this. I'm leaving."

They all agreed with Edna and packed up their stuff, which wasn't much, and headed out into the night.

The next morning, there was no sound of a rooster or even a cow. Farmer Fred looked outside and saw that all the animals were gone.

"Oh no," he said, "all the animals are gone."

Farmer Fred became sad immediately. Now, it was one thing to be serious, but it was another thing to be sad.

Farmer Fred didn't like the feeling at all.

He got into his truck and drove down the road in search of his friends.

He went about four miles, but there was no sign of them anywhere. Then he heard some laughter in the distance.

He followed the sound and saw the animals walking through the woods.

He got out of his truck, walked into the forest, and asked, "What's going on here?"
"We couldn't stand it," said Edna. "We've tried to cheer you up, but nothing's worked, so we're running away. Well, walking away."

The other animals nodded in agreement.

"Well, that's no way to solve a problem," said Farmer Fred. "You don't just leave. I mean, sure, I'm serious, but that doesn't mean you have to be. And, besides, we're family. I take care of you. I need you.

Not to mention that you're safe on the farm. You'd probably be eaten by lions in a day or two out here in the woods."

The animals thought about this for a moment.

As they whispered to one another about the lion issue, Farmer Fred mumbled, "Cows and chickens runnin' wild in the woods, heh, heh."

Edna turned quickly and said, "What was that?"
"I think he laughed a little," said Bernie.
"Yes," said a chicken, "I heard it. It wasn't much, but he did laugh."

"Well," said Edna, "in that case, you're witty enough for us, Farmer Fred. And we care about you, too. I guess we can go back to the farm."

The other animals nodded their heads and said things like "I agree" and "Good idea" and "Let's go back."

They hopped onto the truck and Farmer Fred drove them home.

From that day forward, they were able to make Farmer Fred laugh a little more, especially by bringing up the idea of cows and chickens running wild, although he still doesn't see anything funny about corn.